MW00905818

Angels INC.

Angels INC.

Published simultaneously in 2008 in Great Britain and Canada by Tradewind Books Limited
www.tradewindbooks.com

Distribution in Canada by Publishers Group Canada and Raincoast Books • Distribution in the USA by Orca Book Publishers • Distribution in Australia by John Reed Books • Distribution in the UK by Turnaround

Text copyright © 2008 by Bruce McBay • Illustrations copyright © 2008 by Kim La Fave

All rights reserved. No part of this publication may be reproduced, stored in a retrieval system or transmitted, in any form or by any means, without the prior written permission of the publisher or, in the case of photocopying or other reprographic copying, a license from ACCESS COPYRIGHT, Toronto, Ontario.

The right of Bruce McBay and Kim La Fave to be identified as the author and illustrator of this work has been asserted by them in accordance with the Copyright, Design and Patents Act 1988.

Book design by Elisa Gutiérrez and Jacqueline Wang

10 9 8 7 6 5 4 3 2 1

LIBRARY AND ARCHIVES CANADA CATALOGUING IN PUBLICATION

McBay, Bruce, 1946-

Angels Inc. / by Bruce McBay ; [illustrated by Kim LaFave].

ISBN 978-1-896580-30-2

I. LaFave, Kim II. Title.

PS8575.B39A64 2008
jC813'.54   C2008-902944-5

Printed and bound in Canada

This book has been printed on 100% ancient forest-friendly paper certified by the Forest Stewardship Council (FSC).

y **Bruce McBay** with illustrations by **Kim La Fave**

Vancouver · London

he publisher wishes to thank the Government of Canada and Canadian
eritage for their financial support through the Canada Council for the
rts, the Book Publishing Industry Development Program (BPIDP) and
he Association for the Export of Canadian Books (AECB). The publisher
so wishes to thank the Government of the Province of British Columbia
or the financial support it has extended through the Book Publishing
ax Credit program and the British Columbia Arts Co

 Canada Council   Conseil des Arts
for the Arts   du Canada

 BRITISH
COLUMBIA
ARTS COUNCIL

*To all those earthbound angels who
dedicate their lives to helping others*
—BM

*I'd like to thank James Heneghan with whom
I first developed this story some years back.
I'd also like to thank Kim Aippersbach for
her diligent editing and helpful suggestions.*
—BM

To Pamela
—KL

Chapter 1

IT WAS SATURDAY.
The last Saturday in April. No school. A perfect spring day in Vancouver. The houses on Twenty-First Avenue were quickly drying off from the morning rain. Wendy Appleton walked along thinking of the people living there: Mr. and Mrs. Beale, Mrs. Creech and Mrs. Haddock. She thought it was funny the way houses start to look like their owners. At the end of the street she saw her friend Zachary Plummer waiting for her in front of his house. They were taking the number seven bus to Granville Island like they did every Saturday.

"Say, it's going to be a hot day today. Let's get ice cream," suggested Zach.

"Do you have money?" asked Wendy.

"Yeah, my mom gave me five bucks. Let's spend it!"

When the bus dropped them off, they walked as fast as they could over the causeway to Granville Island. Up ahead they heard a steel-drum band playing loudly. Wendy led the way to the boardwalk triangle in front of the French bakery. They skipped right up to where a crowd was laughing and swaying in time to the music.

"Let's stop and listen," said Wendy, pushing in closer.

"What about our ice cream?" Zach complained.

"Music is the food of the soul, Zach. Forget about your stomach for once."

Zach groaned but followed his friend.

There were five musicians standing behind their steel drums. Their shoulders bounced. Their feet tapped. Their drumsticks moved in a blur. Two of the drummers wore strange hats with bright-blue and orange feathers. The audience was swaying, stomping and smiling to the music.

"Look. There's crabby Mrs. Creech." Zach pointed to the one unsmiling face in the crowd.

"She's not crabby," said Wendy.

"She's always yelling at me," said Zach.

"That's because you always cut across her lawn," said Wendy.

Wendy wanted everyone in the world to be as happy as she was right now. If only she could do something to make Mrs. Creech happy. She watched Mrs. Creech moving about at the back of the crowd. She thought the old woman looked confused.

"She's waiting to cross the street to the market," said Wendy. "But look at that traffic. I bet she's been waiting there for ages. It must be tough being old."

The cars were not moving very fast, but they were bumper to bumper.

"Let's help her across," said Wendy. She walked right in front of the musicians and out through the crowd. Zach sighed and followed her.

Wendy marched right up to Mrs. Creech and grabbed her by one arm. "We'll help you, Mrs. Creech," she said. "Come on, Zach." Zach grabbed Mrs. Creech's other arm, and they started to steer her carefully through the continuous stream of cars.

"Wha...!" cried Mrs. Creech in alarm, struggling feebly.

"It's okay, Mrs. Creech. It's me, Wendy Appleton. I live two doors down from you, you know."

They carried the old woman across the street. Mrs. Creech weighed only about as much as a seagull. Then they placed her gently and safely on the other side near the potted plants and sweet-smelling flowers outside the market entrance.

"B-but..." spluttered Mrs. Creech, waving her skinny arms about like wings. "Take your hands..." She pushed backward, trying to escape. "Arrgh! You b-boys!"

"I'm a girl, Mrs. Creech," said Wendy. "But that's okay. Don't feel bad about it. It's probably my short hair and these old jeans. We're glad we could be of help."

Free at last, Mrs. Creech muttered and cursed and shook her fist at Zach. Dodging skilfully through the traffic, she went back across the street into the crowd and the happy music.

Sheesh! Zach thought. *She didn't really want to cross the road after all. She was just listening to the band.*

"Come on, Zach, let's go get that ice cream," Wendy said. "And then we'll take the bus up to Point Grey to look for other folks to help out."

Chapter 2

A FEW DAYS LATER after school, Wendy and Zach walked over to Sodas for ice cream.

"I enjoyed helping Mrs. Creech," said Wendy between slurps of her butterscotch-liquorice ice-cream cone.

Zach gave a muffled sound. It was hard for him to speak with a triple-decker Death-by-Chocolate Avalanche crammed into his mouth. Finally, after wiping his face neatly with his shirtsleeve, he said, "We should have just left her alone."

"We're supposed to be kind to old folks," said Wendy, shaking her head. "People ought to help people more. It would be a nicer world."

Zach rolled his eyes.

Wendy ignored him. "Let's form a club," she said.

"What kind of club?"

"A club to help people."

"What kind of people?"

"Duh. People who need help," Wendy answered.

Zach stared at her. "You mean you want us to start a club to *help* people?"

"That's right." Wendy fixed him with her no-blink stare. "What about it?"

"What about what?" asked Zach, looking greedily at a kid being handed a Pecan-Fudge Overkill.

"What about my idea?" said Wendy. "A club to help people."

"People should do stuff for themselves," said Zach.

"But some people just can't," argued Wendy.

Zach shrugged.

"Then I'll start a club on my own."

Zach thought about it. He didn't want Wendy to start something up on her own. She was his best friend. They had lived on the same street since kindergarten. "Don't be so quick. I didn't say I *wouldn't* help."

"You'll help? You're a real friend, Zach. You'll have fun, I promise. Didn't it feel good when we helped old Mrs. Creech?"

"No."

"What'll we call our club?"

They thought for a minute. Zach scrunched up his eyebrows. "Club M-I-N-K," he said.

"M-I-N-K? Mink?"

"Meddlesome Interfering Nosy Kids Club."

"Be serious," said Wendy. "Think of something simple, like The Good Deed Club."

"Bo-ooooo-ring," said Zach.

"Well, you come up with something, then."

"How about Angels Inc.?"

"Ink? Like a pen?"

"No, Inc., like *Monsters Inc.*"

"Angels Inc. I like it!"

Chapter 3

ON SATURDAY EVENING the two Angels watched TV and ate popcorn at Wendy's place. Zach was lying on the floor with his arm resting on a cushion. Wendy's legs were sprawled all over the couch.

"Our next mission," announced Wendy, "is Mr. Beale's potting shed."

"What's the matter with it?" asked Zach.

"It needs new paint."

"Which one is Mr. Beale?" asked Zach, who could never remember the names of the people on their street.

"Stupid. The Beales are the couple next door with all the flowers," Wendy explained. "My dad is always complaining that their shed is a disgrace to the neighbourhood. It's all run-down and old-looking. It hasn't been painted in ages."

Zach was horrified. "You want *us* to paint the shed?"

"Why not?" said Wendy. "It'll be fun. And think what a nice surprise they'll get."

"Let's leave that job until we have more members in the club," said Zach. "Many hands make light work."

"My dad's got lots of leftover paint in our garage," said Wendy, ignoring Zach's suggestion.

"It's been there for years. We'd be doing my dad a favour by using it up."

"My dad has a few rollers and brushes in the garage," Zach said with resignation. "And I'm sure there are a few cans of leftover paint."

"So it's all set then?" asked Wendy.

"Sure," answered Zach with a sigh. "But how can we paint their shed and make it a surprise for them if they're watching us from their kitchen window?"

"I happen to know," said Wendy, "that Dunbar Community Centre is running an all-day bus trip to the tulip festival in Lynden, Washington next Saturday. The Beales are going with my gran. Which means we'll have all day to paint the shed."

Which is what they did.

The next Saturday was warm and sunny. A perfect day for painting. Zach came down the alley to the Beales' house carrying several cans of paint, two rollers and a tray. Wendy opened the gate for him. There were six cans of paint of various colours lined up near the potting shed.

"Are you sure about this?" asked Zach. "Do we even have enough paint?"

Wendy inspected the cans. "There's half a can of blue and an almost-full can of green. Then

there's two yellow ones about three-quarters full. And there's half a can of this mustardy colour and a quarter can of orange."

"I've got two reds and half a can of green," said Zach, "and a pink and a brown and a black."

"That's not black, it's purple."

"If we mix these all together they'll turn into pukey brown," said Zach.

"Why do we have to mix them? Why not make the shed rainbow-coloured?"

Zach looked at the shed. It was very old. The original paint was worn off, and the wood was now a weathered grey. It certainly did need brightening up. He shrugged. "Sounds like a good idea. Let's get started."

Wendy and Zach worked most of the morning, shaking and mixing, bending and stretching, reaching and leaning, brushing and rolling. They painted squares and triangles and circles, each a different colour. "Variety is the spice of life," said Zach.

Every so often, Wendy stood back and inspected the shed. "It's just beautiful," she said.

Zach had to admit that Wendy was right. The shed shimmered and shone in its bright new colours.

They were finished by lunchtime. The two Angels had almost as much paint on their clothes as was on the shed.

"The Beales will be so happy," said Wendy. "What a surprise they'll get when they see their old shed. They won't recognize it."

"Well," said Zach, looking from the brightly coloured shed to the Beales' plain white house, "they'll definitely be surprised."

After Wendy and Zach cleaned up, they heard voices through the hedge next door.

"Hey, look. Who's that?" said Wendy.

A man and a woman were peering into Mrs. Creech's garage. The man was short and fat and dressed in a dark coat. The woman was bigger than the man and wore a pink jogging suit.

"Haven't seen them before," said Zach.

"No," said Wendy. "Wonder what they're up to?"

The man turned their way, and Wendy smiled and waved at him. He scowled, grabbed the woman's arm and hurried them both down the alleyway.

"That was weird," said Wendy.

"I bet they were thieves and we scared them off," said Zach. "That's two good deeds for today!"

"Hmm," said Wendy. "I wonder."

"Are you coming to my house for lunch?" asked Zach.

"Right," said Wendy. "I'm starving!"

Chapter 4

ON THE WAY TO SCHOOL on Monday, Zach asked Wendy how the Beales had liked their shed.

"They loved it. I watched them through the window when the bus dropped them off yesterday evening. They couldn't believe their eyes."

"Oh yeah?" Zach grinned.

"They danced around it for the longest time, waving their arms about, singing and yelling like you wouldn't believe. They were so happy."

After school, the two friends sat at a beat-up old table in Wendy's backyard.

"Now that Angels Inc. is so successful, we should elect a president," said Wendy.

"President?" said Zach. "Why do we need a president when there's only two people in the club?"

"Because every club has a president, that's why. And since it was my idea, I think it should be me."

"We have to vote for the president," said Zach. "Why should I vote for you?"

"If you vote for me I promise to have lots of breaks for snacks and ice cream."

"Okay. You're the president."

"Thanks."

"You're welcome."

Wendy cleared her throat. "Ahem. As President of Angels Inc., I propose that we complete one mission every Saturday."

"Every Saturday!" groaned Zach. "You want me to spend every single Saturday doing good deeds? What about our trips to Granville Island for ice cream?"

"We can still go to Granville Island. It will be our reward."

"Okay," said Zach. "Remember, you promised ice cream when we elected you president."

"True," said Wendy. "Tell you what: next Saturday we'll go for ice cream and then we can decide what our good deed will be."

"It's a deal," said Zach.

Chapter 5

OUTSIDE THE MARKET on the following Saturday, Wendy stopped to take a deep sniff of the flowers.

"Come on," said Zach. "Our ice cream awaits."

"Sometimes you have to stop and smell the flowers," said Wendy. A toy poodle stopped and smelled Zach's old sneakers.

"Hey," said Wendy. "Don't we know this dog?"

Zach said, "Hello, little dog." He patted it carefully. The dog had a funny hairdo.

At the other end of her leash stood a tall woman in high heels, wearing a smart red jacket, reading the sign outside the market door: NO DOGS ALLOWED EXCEPT GUIDE DOGS. "Oh, dear!" she said in a fluster.

"Hi, Mrs. Haddock!" said Wendy. "What's wrong?"

Mrs. Haddock was very upset. "I must pick up Pooky's birthday cake at the market bakery, but I can't take him inside."

Zach pointed to a bored Doberman sitting coolly near the flowers, its leash tied to a bicycle stand. "You could leave Pukey outside, like that dog."

"Pooky, not Pukey!" the woman angrily corrected him. She turned to Wendy. "Pooky would cry and cry," she said. "Besides, somebody could steal him away! What am I to do?"

"We'll take care of your dog for you," said Wendy. "Pooky is safe with us."

Mrs. Haddock didn't look like she wanted to leave her little Pooky in their hands.

"Would you take good care of him?"

"Sure," said Wendy confidently. "Go pick up your cake. We'll be right here with Pooky when you get back."

"Very well." Mrs. Haddock handed the leash to Wendy. "It's Pooky's birthday tomorrow and he must have his cake." She bent down to talk to her pet. "Momsy be gone for oney a liddle minute, Pooky Wookums." She patted the dog on the top of its head and disappeared into the market.

Wendy handed the leash to Zach. "Pooky Wookums seems to like your smelly old sneakers, Zach."

Zach said, "If she pays us for our dog-minding services, we could get more ice cream."

Wendy was horrified. "We're Angels Inc., remember? We don't take pay for a good deed."

Zach sighed, but then he brightened up. "That's right: this is our good deed for the day, isn't it?"

"I suppose so," said Wendy. "That was easy!"

"Easier than painting sheds," muttered Zach.

While Wendy and Zach were talking, Pooky finished with Zach's sneakers and wandered over to the bored Doberman. Pooky sniffed the Doberman. The Doberman was not in the mood to be sniffed at by a dog not much bigger than a half-grown rabbit. He let out a great hollow bark and jumped up, showing Pooky his fine pointed teeth.

Pooky was badly frightened by this unfriendly display. He jerked the leash from Zach's fingers, tumbled through a deep puddle and fled across the street. The Doberman jumped after Pooky, snapping the leather leash as though it were only cotton thread. Both dogs disappeared into a crowd of people gathered around a juggler.

"After them!" yelled Wendy.

The two Angels threw themselves into the crowd. People scattered in confusion.

"Look out!" yelled Zach.

Chapter 6

THE TWO DOGS charged right toward the juggler. He had three white balls, two bowling pins and a green watering can sailing through the air around him. When he saw the dogs he tried to back out of the way, but Pooky ran between his legs and the Doberman dodged around him, tripping his feet and making him fall onto his bum. Balls, bowling pins and watering can came crashing to the ground.

The terrified poodle darted past the bakery and across the parking lot into the boat yard, the grinning Doberman close on his heels.

Wendy dashed after the dogs yelling "Pooky!" at the top of her voice. Zach threw two of the balls back to the juggler before the juggler started chasing him. Then Zach ran after Wendy and Pooky and the Doberman.

Pooky scampered under a boat, around a hoist and through a sawhorse. The Doberman charged after him, scattering boat yard workmen and knocking over paint cans. Then Pooky skidded across the grass by the seawall and slid into a deep muddy puddle.

The Doberman had him.

"Leave that poor little dog alone, you big bully!" Wendy yelled at the Doberman.

But Pooky was all right. The Doberman bent its great grinning head down into the puddle and fished Pooky out. Then he began licking the thick mud off the poodle's startled face. Both dogs' tails were wagging.

"Pick him up, Zach."

Zach looked at the Doberman's fine set of teeth. "No, you pick him up."

"You're not scared, are you, Zach?"

"Who me? Scared? You gotta be kidding." Zach bent down, his hands reaching for the poodle.

The Doberman had other ideas. He nipped Pooky playfully on the tail. With a happy yip-yap, Pooky jumped up and took off, splashing back through the muddy puddle.

Zach pounced on the puppy. "Got the little sucker!"

"Good work, Zach!" said Wendy.

"Woof!" said the Doberman. Trailing his broken leash, he followed them happily back to the lane outside the market.

Mrs. Haddock was standing beside the flowers holding a huge cake box, looking frantic.

When she saw them she gasped. "My poor Pooky! What have they done to you?"

Balancing the cake box in one hand, she reached out and scooped Pooky into her arms. When she saw the mud smeared on her smart red jacket, she screamed and dropped the box containing the birthday cake.

Zach quickly bent down and picked it up. "Here," he said, handing it back to Mrs. Haddock. "Don't worry, it hardly got squashed at all."

The woman glared angrily at the two Angels. "I would like to give you two children a piece of my—"

"Oh, that's okay," said Wendy. "You don't need to give us anything. We were glad to be of help. And we had fun taking care of your dog."

Mrs. Haddock spluttered and gasped. Then she marched away shaking her head so angrily her cheeks wobbled like jello.

"Goodbye, Pooky!" called Wendy. She turned to Zach. "Well, that's another mission accomplished by Angels Inc.," she said proudly. "Just think—if more and more people join our new club and do more and more good deeds, why...it will spread all around the world." She held out her arms. "All around the world!"

"Boggles the mind," mumbled Zach, wiping mud off his hoodie.

Chapter 7

THE NEXT MEETING of Angels Inc. was Monday after school on a beat-up old sofa in Zach's basement.

"What's our first item of business?" asked Wendy.

"A double order of jelly doughnuts and a case of pop."

"No," said Wendy firmly. "Business first and snack later. Now, any ideas for a mission?"

They sat thinking for several minutes. Wendy said, "Perhaps we could offer to mow Mrs. Creech's front lawn. It hasn't been done since last year."

"No! Not Mrs. Creech again!"

"She's very old and can't do it herself. Everything's very overgrown."

"Wendy, she'll take one look at us and yell for the police. Isn't it enough that we frightened her out of her mind at Granville Market?"

"Oh, we did not!" cried Wendy. "You just don't want to mow her lawn."

"But she won't appreciate it," Zach protested. "What's the good of doing something for someone if it's not going to be appreciated?"

"An Angel shouldn't expect thanks. It should be..." Wendy searched for the right words.

"A pure act, selfless, without any reward?" suggested Zach.

"That's it. Pure act. I like that."

"The only reward is the feeling of joy that comes from helping your neighbour?" asked Zach. "Is that what you mean?"

"You're sure good with words, Zach. Yes, that's exactly what I was trying to say. Thanks."

"You're welcome."

"Then it's a go?"

"No. I don't get a feeling of joy when I work for nothing."

"Zachary!"

"What?"

"We're in this together. We're friends!"

"Oh, all right," agreed Zach with a shrug and a sigh. "Say, maybe my dad will let us use his new Supermow 3000!"

Saturday morning they headed up the sidewalk to Mrs. Creech's house dragging the new lawnmower from Zach's garage.

Zach stared at the mower. "Even with this fancy machine it's going to be tough getting through Mrs. Creech's grass. It's like taking a pair of scissors to the Amazon jungle."

"At least your dad let you bring his new Supermow."

"He didn't know the Creech place is so overgrown. I just hope the digitally balanced rotors won't get damaged."

As they approached Mrs. Creech's yard, a truck pulled up in front of her house. A man and a woman got out. The man was short and fat, in a dark suit and tie. The woman was bigger than the man and wore a smart pink pant suit. Her lips were painted a very

bright red. Wendy put out her hand to stop
Zach.

"What?" said Zach.

"Shhhh!" whispered Wendy. "That's the same people we saw snooping around Mrs. Creech's garage." She pulled Zach toward Mr. Beale's shed, and they peered around the edge of it.

"This is going to be our best score yet!" said the man. "Is the truck big enough?"

"I think so," said the woman. "There's a lot of junk mixed in with the good stuff. We don't need to take it all."

They went up the walk and rang Mrs. Creech's front door.

"They're up to no good," said Wendy. "I think you're right: I think they're thieves."

Chapter 8

ZACH AND WENDY slipped along the side of the hedge so they could hear what was being said when Mrs. Creech opened the door.

"Hello," they heard the large pink woman say. "We're from the Helping Hand Foundation. We're the ones who phoned you last week about cleaning out your garage."

"Oh, wonderful," said Mrs. Creech. "It's so cluttered with all my junk, I could never have tackled it on my own. You can bring your truck around back. I've left the garage door open for you."

"We'll get started right away," said the woman.

The man and woman quickly walked back to their truck.

"I think we should warn Mrs. Creech," said Wendy. "They're crooks, all right. I'm sure of it."

"You warn Mrs. Creech. I don't want to get yelled at!"

Wendy stared at him. "I thought we were in this together. Remember? Angels Inc.? And I'm the president!"

"Okay, okay."

They pushed through the hedge, climbed the creaky steps and knocked on Mrs. Creech's door.

Mrs. Creech's head appeared. She was wearing large round glasses that made her look like an owl.

"Well? What do you children want?"

"Mrs. Creech, did you just give a man and a woman permission to clean out your garage?" asked Wendy.

"Yes, they're from a very good organization, helping seniors like myself to keep things tidy."

"We think they're thieves. We heard them say that there were valuable things in the garage," said Wendy.

"What?" said Mrs. Creech. "Now you listen here, Wendy Appleton! Who do you think you are, accusing respectable people of being crooks?"

"But they are," said Zach. "We heard them."

"Eavesdropping, is that what you were doing?" asked Mrs. Creech.

"No, no, not on purpose," said Zach.

"We're just trying to help," Wendy explained. "We're Angels Inc. That's what we do. We take care of people's dogs, we paint sheds, we..."

"So that was *you*, was it?" cried Mrs. Creech. "Mr. and Mrs. Beale are absolutely furious about that shed. It's hideous!"

"No it's not," protested Zach feebly.

"And it was you who let poor Pooky run away and get filthy muddy last week. Mrs. Haddock was in tears when she got back from Granville Island. You ruined her best coat and destroyed her fancy cake."

"But, but..." said Wendy.

"And you're the ones who carried me across the street when I didn't want to go. You are a couple of meddlesome interfering kids, and you have no idea what you're talking about! You get away from here this instant, before you do any more damage!"

"But..."

"Come on, Wendy," Zach said. "We'd better go."

Wendy was about to start crying. She let Zach take her arm and pull her down the walk and back to where they had left the lawnmower.

"We were trying to help!" sobbed Wendy, tears spilling down her cheeks. "She said we just ruined everything. Didn't we do any good at all?"

"Um, sure we did," said Zach, patting her arm. "After all, it's the thought that counts."

Wendy sniffed and wiped her eyes. "Well, Angel's Inc. is going to do something right for a change! We're going to catch those crooks in the act! Come on, Zach!"

Zach rolled his eyes, shook his head and followed Wendy.

They snuck through Mr. Beale's yard and crouched behind his back fence. The truck was parked in the alleyway in front of Mrs. Creech's garage.

They saw the man and woman come out of the garage carrying an old brass lamp.

"I bet that's a valuable antique," whispered Wendy. "We have to do something!"

"Why should we?" said Zach. "You heard her. She's happy they're taking away her stuff."

"Zach, there's a crime being committed here!"

"Yeah—my time's being wasted!"

"That's not all that's going to be wasted if you don't come up with an idea to stop these crooks."

"Okay, okay!" They thought for several minutes while a bumblebee hummed lazily through Mr. Beale's flowerbed and the crooks went back into the garage for another load.

"I've got it!" said Zach. "Crooks always have to make fast getaways!"

"Yeah," Wendy said.

"So let's not let them!" Zach said. "If we can get the keys from the truck, they won't get away!"

Chapter 9

ZACH AND WENDY snuck up to the man and woman's truck.

"There's a dog in there," said Zach, backing away.

Wendy said, "It's a collie. They're usually friendly."

They tried the driver's door. It was unlocked. Wendy said, "Hello, big dog." She smiled her

friendliest smile. The dog smiled back and wagged his tail. Wendy climbed in behind the wheel.

"The keys should just be hanging in the ignition," said Zach. "Grab them, and let's get out of here!"

Wendy reached around the steering wheel, feeling for the keys. The dog stuck its nose into her ear.

"Hey, cut that out!" she said. "They're not here!" she whispered back to Zach.

"Are you sure?" Zach hurried around to the passenger door and climbed in. "We've got to hurry. Those crooks could come back any second."

The collie was overjoyed with his new friends. He leaped into Zach's lap and started licking his face and making little dancing movements with his front paws. Zach shoved the dog off his lap onto Wendy and leaned over to look under the steering wheel.

Wendy spluttered and fumbled. "Get off me, you stupid great dog!" she cried.

The dog jumped on Zach, knocking him off the seat. Zach grabbed out blindly. He pulled, and something clicked.

"Zach!"

"What?" Zach was now on the floor beneath the dog.

"We're moving!"

"What?"

"Get up! Look!"

The truck was rolling slowly down the alley. Right toward Mr. Beale's garbage cans.

"Quick! Put your foot on the brake!" Zach yelled.

Wendy tried to reach the brake with her foot, but the dog was in the way.

"Oh, no..."

Crash! They banged into the garbage cans. That didn't slow them down. They rolled past Wendy's house.

"Keep it straight!" yelled Zach.

"I can't see!" screamed Wendy.

"We're headed right for those trees!"

The truck swerved and bounced, hit two more cans, then bumped over some muddy ruts at the end of the alleyway and shuddered to a halt.

"Oh, thank goodness!" said Wendy.

"Let's bail!" said Zach. "We're going to be in trouble!"

They pushed hard on the truck doors and fell

out into the mud. The dog jumped out and started barking. They saw the man and woman puffing down the alley, waving and yelling.

"Run!" yelled Wendy. "Head for the trees!"

Soon Wendy and Zach were out of sight, deep in the woods.

"That was a real close one," said Zach.

"Come on," said Wendy. "Let's sneak back around my house and see what they're doing."

They crouched behind Wendy's fence and peered out. The man and woman were up to their ankles in mud, trying to push their truck out of the ditch while the dog jumped about, barking and getting in the way.

"Hey, you kids! What's going on?" Zach and Wendy jumped. It was Mr. Beale. He had come out to his backyard to see what the noise was about.

"Those two people are thieves!" said Wendy. "That truck is full of stuff they stole from Mrs. Creech's garage." She told Mr. Beale about everything that had happened.

"I've heard of these scam artists," said Mr. Beale. "They've been targeting seniors all over

Vancouver. And here I was going to call a tow truck to get them out of the ditch. I'll call the police instead!"

In a few minutes, the police arrived. The collie greeted them happily, but the crooks ran off into the woods. "Look! They're getting away!" said Wendy.

"They won't get far," said Mr. Beale. "Those crooks have cheated their last victim."

Epilogue

THE NEXT SATURDAY Mrs. Creech invited Wendy and Zach for a snack after they mowed her lawn.

"You make good cookies Mrs. Creech," said Zach, helping himself to his seventh one.

"It's the least I could do. Are you sure I can't pay you for cutting my lawn?"

"No. We're Angels Inc.," said Wendy.

"It's a good thing you warned me about those crooks. Who'd have guessed that the antiques in my garage are worth so much money."

"It's our job to help people," Wendy said.

"Does that include painting?" asked Mr. Beale, as he walked into the kitchen. "Somebody made a mess of my shed."

Wendy and Zach avoided his eyes.

"Um..." said Zach.

"We'd be happy to paint your shed, right, Zach?" said Wendy.

"Okay," said Zach with a sigh. "Can't think of anything I'd rather do."

Bruce McBay was an English teacher
in Burnaby, BC for many years.
He co-wrote *Nannycatch Chronicles* and
Waiting for Sarah with James Heneghan.

Kim La Fave has won many awards
including the Governor General's
Award, the Ruth Swartz Children's
Book Award and the Amelia Frances
Howard-Gibbon Award. He lives in
Gibsons, BC with his family.

Visit the **Angels Inc**. blog and log your own good deeds!
http://angelsinc.wordpress.com/